# Colton Mac

# TWISTED TALES

To order additional copies of this book, contact:
Xlibris
844-714-8691
www.Xlibris.com
Orders@Xlibris.com

ISBN:    Softcover        979-8-3694-1201-5
         EBook            979-8-3694-1200-8

Library of Congress Control Number: 2023922265

Print information available on the last page

Rev. date: 11/22/2023

# TWISTED TALES

# JAMES

James walked into a public bathroom in the middle of the night with tears running down his face. He made his way into one of the stalls and sat down on the toilet. He began to rock back and forth while mumbling words to himself and smacking his head. He continued to do that for several minutes until he got himself under control. Then he pulled out a piece of paper and pen and began to write.

Dear family,

Today was supposed to be an amazing day for me. I have been clean for six months now. None of you seem to care that I am. I understand I have relapsed several times, lied to you all, and have robbed you. But for the first time since I was eighteen, I have not done any drugs in six months.

You all just push me away. None of you will help me get back on my feet. I never asked for money. All I asked was to live with you for a few months so I can get back on my feet. All of you say you don't have time for my games. None of you will let me see your kids for you don't want them to be around my lifestyle. It tears my heart apart for I have not seen most of them before.

But I apologize that I have been a burden in your lives. None of you will have to deal with me anymore. I just hope that Mom and Dad are more welcoming to me when I get to them. I sure do miss them—Dad's big hugs and Mom's warm smiles.

James put down the paper, looking down upon it with tears running down his face. He wiped them away and took one more deep breath, and then he pulled out a needle with gasoline in it. He pulled up his sleeve, took off his belt, and wrapped it around his arm above his elbow, making his veins pop out of his skin. Then he put the needle into his vein, looked up to the ceiling, took a deep breath, looked down at his arm, and injected the gasoline into his veins.

He slowly pulled out a lighter and lit it. As his hand slowly moved, his arm and his hand began to shake. Once the lighter touched where he put the needle in, the flame was sucked into his arm. His veins lit up bright orange and fire spread through his whole body.

After just a few seconds of watching it, he began to sweat like crazy. He panicked and headed out of the stall where he fell to his knees, grabbing his face and screaming. Then flames burst from his eyeballs and melted down his face. James begged for it to stop, to let him die, as he made his way to the door. With all the pain and not being able to see, he could not find the door handle. He slammed his body against the door trying to break out—until his body collapsed. James's body started to twitch as his soul left his body and his clothes caught on fire.

#  PUPPY

Two sisters, Ava and Mia, were hanging out at Mia's house while their husbands were out playing golf. They had two little boys, Sam and Jack, who were the same age playing in the backyard with the two pit bulls and an English mastiff. The sisters were in the kitchen drinking coffee and gossiping about their lives and what was new in them.

Later, as the sun was setting, Ava went out to the backyard to get her son Sam. She looked everywhere and could not find him. She began to panic, running through the backyard screaming her son's name. She looked under everything, even seeing if there was a hole in the fence for him to get out of the backyard in any way possible.

After a while, Mia came out with her son Jack to see what was going on. "Sis, is everything OK? Where is Sam?"

"I can't find him! He is missing!" Ava shouted.

"Jack, did Sam leave the backyard?" asked Mia as her voice began to crack. She too was getting nervous.

The boy just shook his head no but would not speak as if afraid of something. Mia pulled the boy close, holding him tightly so he could not move. Mia ran inside with Jack and called the police. As she did, she looked outside and noticed the English mastiff was just staring at them from the yard. But something about him felt off.

The police arrived and the husbands were right behind them. The police began to ask their questions to the parents. As Mia was standing in the kitchen listening, she noticed the mastiff had not moved from its earlier spot.

The two pit bulls were whimpering across the yard.

After several hours of questioning everyone in the neighborhood, the police left. But they still manned several checkpoints for cars driving through.

At almost 3:00 a.m., Mia convinced Ava to come in and rest and let the police do their job. Both husbands were at the house getting flyers ready.

As Ava lay down on a couch, her husband put a blankie over her. "Get some rest, love. We will drive around the neighborhood and keep looking," he said.

As Ava pulled the blanket tightly around her, both men headed out. Mia gave Ava an extra pillow and helped her get more comfortable before heading up the stairs. Ava lay on the couch for a couple of hours before she finally passed out.

The next morning, Mia made a pot of coffee and woke up Ava and her husband to keep the search going. Ava stretched and headed to the kitchen, and her husband was in the bathroom when she heard a dog yelping in the backyard. Ava ran to the window to see what was going on. She saw the English mastiff running around in circles trying to get rid of some shit that was stuck in his butt.

She ran out there in her pajamas, grabbed hold of the dog, pulled a Kleenex from her pocket, and then tried to pull the shit out. It was white and sticky. She pulled and pulled, but it wouldn't give. She finally yanked hard, and this time it gave just a little. She noticed something very strange.

It started to look like a hand. As she pulled harder and harder, more and more came out. The blood began to leave her face as she feared the dog had eaten the child.

When his head came out, she dropped and screamed. Her husband came running out to see what was going on.

He immediately fell to his knees in shock as the dog ran in circles trying to get the body out of him.

After a while, the boy fell out and the body lay in the middle of the yard. The dog walked over to lick him, and the mother lost her mind. "Get away from him!" she screamed.

The dog ran in fear to the corner of the yard, whimpering confused about what he did. The mother screamed while holding her child, and the father was too petrified to move.

The sounds of sirens could be heard, and the neighbors came running over to see what was going on.

Eventually the cops took the dog away to be put down as the boy's body was taken to the morgue.

The family got ready to visit their son one last time. The drive seemed to take forever to get there. Their bodies felt heavy as they got out of the car, every step harder than the last one.

As they entered the building, they rang the front desk's bell several times, but no one came. Ava finally lost her patience and headed around the desk to the back. The rest of them followed without question. As they opened the door to the back, they saw a long, black hall. The only light, at the end of the hallway, was from another room. As they made their way down the hall, they were all getting goosebumps.

When they opened the door to the room, they saw their son on the wall being held up by spider webs. Thousands of spiders were crawling around him. When there was a giant thud, all jumped and screamed. As they turned in horror, the funeral director's body was on the ground ripped open. On the ceiling was a giant spider slowly eating a hand.

# BERSERKERS

I t was a cold October night in the middle of a forest and young adults were partying at a cabin, drinking beer, taking shots, and having a great time. They had a giant fire going, lighting up the back of the cabin. Three of them were drinking some beers around the fire. Two were on the deck, while the other five were inside dancing and taking shots.

Suddenly a young man came running out of the forest screaming for help. One of the guys grabbed an axe and took a step forward while the other two stepped back. As he came out of the forest into the light from the fire, he was covered in blood with one of his eyes hanging out. The two girls on the deck ran inside to get the others.

He fell to his knees breathing heavily as blood dripped off his body onto the ground. He looked up at them and said, "Run." Taking his last breath, he fell on the ground.

As the man with the axe walked up slowly to see if he was alive, the rest of the group came walking out to the deck to see what was going. Someone on the deck yelled, "Be careful!" when a male moose head and its spine came flying out of the forest, landing in the fire and causing it to splatter everywhere.

The ones on the deck screamed and a couple of them even fell backward. While two of the guys down there ran back to the cabin for safety, the other one was too close to the fire and became enflamed. The two friends panicked and ran over to help as he was rolling on the ground. They patted him down, killing the fire, but not before it gave him third-degree burns over most of his body.

As he lay on the ground screaming in pain, everyone came running down to see him. One of the girls screamed in horror as she saw him, and one of the guys threw up at the smell of everything. As everyone was worried about their friend, one of them walked over to the fire and stared at the moose's head as the skin melted off and into the fire.

As they picked him up and carried him into the house, they heard a high-pitch scream of something horrible that caused them to flinch. They all looked back at the direction it came from when they noticed something was standing in the shadows with dark-red eyes looking right at them. It took a step closer, and the light flickered off its body, showing more details of the monster.

It had a grin that went from ear to ear with sharp teeth, and they could see human flesh stuck between its teeth. It stood over six feet tall with a pale, naked body. Its fingers where long and sharp with blood dripping off them. Its legs looked like a deer's, with one of them having a gash showing its muscles. Out of its back came several antlers that were covered in moss, and a giant rack with human skin was on it.

The man with the axe tightened his grip. As several others panicked, they dropped their friend and ran inside while the rest dragged him up the deck to get him inside. The man with the axe ran toward the creature, but it hopped right over the young man and went after the others. The rest of the group dropped the burned man, leaving him on the deck as they ran inside and locked the door.

The creature landed on the deck and grabbed the man who was burned, staring at everyone inside as it took a lick of the man's head before biting it off. It chewed slowly while staring and walking slowly toward them.

As the man with the axe came up the stairs screaming, the creature used the headless body to hit him, sending him flying off the deck to the ground, killing him on impact. The creature looked back at them and let out a giant scream that vibrated the windows till they shattered. The pitch of the scream caused them all to fall to their knees and become disoriented.

The creature walked into the house with blood dripping from its body. It grabbed two of the girls and dragged them to the deck. The monster jumped off the deck with the girls and into the air, leaving the last five people on floor trying to get up.

As they were able to finally get up, the last chick wanted to go after them but the guys grabbed their stuff and then headed to the car. She screamed at them as they were loading the car when suddenly two heads hit the ground. They all looked up at the roof to see the creature on the ridge smiling at them as its long tongue licked its face.

As they climbed into the car, the driver hit the gas before the last one could get in, running him over and leaving him in the driveway. As the friends looked back, they saw him screaming in pain. The creature landed on him, causing his body to explode across the drive away.

They sped down the dirt road, not even slowing down for turns. As they all kept looking behind them, they saw the creature chasing them, screaming at them as they tried to get away.

As they went around the last bend before there'd be a straight shot to the main highway, a young woman covered in blood was standing in the middle of the road. The driver panicked, causing him to swerve off the road and into a tree, killing him and the front passenger instantly. This left the three in the back alive. They crawled out of the car as two were OK and other was bleeding from his head and his eye popped out of its eye socket. As they looked at the young woman in the middle of the road staring at them with tears running down her face, she was about to open her mouth when the creature rammed its antlers right into her, vanishing into the night.

The three ran into the forest. The man who was bleeding everywhere ran off on his own screaming. The other two tried to make it to the highway, but before they got there, the creature was standing in front of them, breathing heavily. The two froze, too scared to move. When the man stepped on a twig, the creature screamed, grabbed the man, tossed him into the air, and ripped him apart, causing blood to go all over and cover the young lady in blood.

The creature went down on all four legs and began to walk slowly toward her when it heard the young man screaming in the background. It looked up, screamed, and ran off into the forest to get him. She stood there in shock, unable to move for several hours till she heard a car coming.

She slowly made her way to the road. As she walked onto the road, she was blinded by bright lights until the car swerved off the road and hit a tree. She looked at them as three passengers got out of the car. One had his eye popped out, and the other two were fine. As she looked closely, she saw herself and began to cry. Before she could say anything, the creature stabbed her with its antlers and ran into the night.

# BEAUTIFUL BABY

t was just a normal night for Susan, who was feet five tall with red hair and green eyes, as she came home from a long day of work. Her cat met her at the door, wanting to be fed. Susan chuckled at her little cat and slowly made her way to the kitchen, where she grabbed the food and fed her little cat. She got a text from her friends asking if she was still coming out that night. She rubbed her cat's head and then headed out the door to meet with her friends.

It was almost ten o'clock when she finally arrived at the bar where her friends Kate and Sara were waiting. Sara was five feet tall with long, blonde hair and blue eyes. Kate was about six feet tall with black hair and brown eyes. They got excited when she showed up and they did their own little dance as they entered the bar.

Inside, men kept buying them shots. Within an hour, all three girls were drunk, dancing and singing on the bar top. As the girls got to the point that they were having a hard time standing, the bartender ordered them a cab. As they got into the car giggling and laughing about the night, suddenly hands came out from behind the seat and held them down, covering their mouths with rags. All three girls soon passed out.

Susan woke up to see she was tied by her ankles and wrists to two trees, where she was an inch off the ground. Her heart began to race when she noticed her two friends were across from her and tied up as well. Susan called their names. After shouting their names, they finally came to and began to panic. Before they could say anything, a group of hooded figures came out of the darkness while chanting words that were not English.

As they formed a giant circle around the girls, the girls began shouting back at them to be let go. None of the hooded figures moved. They just continued chanting words, when three of them left the circle, walked up behind them, and pulled out their cocks. All three women began to scream once they figured out what was about to happen to them.

The chanting started to get louder, and they began to rape the women. As the chanting got louder and louder, the three males did it harder. The chanting stopped all at once. And the three males pulled out and walked back in the circle. Then there was silence, and in that moment, the only thing that could be heard was the women crying.

After a minute of silence, Kate screamed in pain. The other two looked over to see Kate's stomach growing bigger and bigger until it burst open and a little baby came falling out. The baby was all red with a tail and horns. Only seconds after that, the other two women had the same experience, delivering devil babies too. The hooded men walked over and picked up the babies, leaving the women tied up with their insides all over the ground.

They quietly walked through the woods and out to an open field, and then they walked to a barn. The three with the babies walked into the barn, where several women naked with six nipples and goats' heads were breastfeeding the handful of other baby devils too.

# SMILING JACK

t was a nice summer afternoon when six teenagers were heading up the mountain. The road followed the mountainside, weaving in and out. The teenagers were goofing off, riding four-wheelers around the bends seeing who could go the fastest and closest to the edge.

Once they reached the mountaintop, they parked. There were two girls and four boys. They set up the fire as the sun was setting. They were joking around the campfire and pulling out stuff to make some s'mores.

They were all having a good time until Jake brought up Smiling Jack. The whole group went quiet, except Rex. Rex was confused as to why the whole group got scared.

"Who is Smiling Jack?" asked Rex, starting to get nervous by the look of fear on his friends' faces.

"You don't know who Smiling Jack is?" asked Alice.

"Smiling Jack was a serial killer back in the eighties," said Ben with a depressed look on his face. "He killed his entire block one night when they had a Halloween party. Poisoned the fruit punch. He said that he got a message from God that he did not want his people to suffer and asked Smiling Jack to save them. The rest of the town didn't agree to that and wanted him dead so they chased him up this mountain to a little pond only a couple of miles from us. They threw him into the pond and drowned him. The rumors are that they left his body in the pond tied to an anchor."

"But why do they call him Smiling Jack?" asked Rex as his voice got squeaky from hearing the story.

"They call him Smiling Jack because he was wearing a wooden mask that had a giant smile on it–like a carved pumpkin. And they threw that mask in the pond with him as he sunk to the bottom," said Ben.

"The tale goes if you throw a nickel into the pond, he will come and take you to his happy place, where you won't suffer anymore and be at peace," said Carol.

"Oh, come on, guys. It's just a campfire story to scare us before we go to bed," said Jake with a grin on his face.

"It doesn't matter what it is. We agreed to not go there. We promised we wouldn't," said Lucy, who was getting irritated with everyone.

"I kind of want to go check out the pond, to be honest," said Rex, trying to look cool for the girls once he noticed they were scared.

"That's my boy. Hell yeah! Let's go!" shouted Jake, standing up.

Both Jake and Rex hopped on their four-wheelers, spinning their tires as they left the campground.

They drove for a half a mile until they got to an off-road trail that you could easily miss if you didn't know it existed. They turned down it and rode till they reached the end, where a small pond was. They hopped off their four-wheelers and walked to the edge of the pond.

"Shall we throw a nickel in the pond and see what happens?" asked Jake, pulling out a nickel from his pocket. He was grinning.

Rex chuckled and nodded at him. Jake threw the nickel into the middle of the pond, making a small splash. They sat and waited for what seemed like forever. Jake finally gave up and headed over to his four-wheeler, but Rex stayed staring at the pond.

Jake started his four-wheeler and hit the throttle a few times, telling Rex to come and leave. As Rex stood up and began to head to his four-wheeler, Jake's face went as pale as a white sheet. Rex turned around to see Smiling Jack himself standing at the edge of the pond.

He was six feet tall and had long, black hair down to his shoulders. He was wearing his wooden mask, with eyes black as night and cracks all over it plus a pitch-black smile that looked like a carved pumpkin's. From his right arm, the anchor dangled on a chain. He was wearing a black cloth like the grim reaper's; the only skin showing were his fingers. They were nothing but rotten flesh with parts of bones exposed.

Rex went pale as he saw Smiling Jack and was frozen out of fear. Smiling Jack lifted his left arm up and pointed his index finger at Rex as puss dripped down. He made a loud moaning before he swung the anchor at Rex, cutting off his head.

Jake snapped out of it once he saw the head rolling on the ground. He quickly spun his four-wheeler around and headed back to his friends. Smiling Jack slowly walked out of the water as the anchor came back to his arm. Smiling Jack walked up the Rex's head and closed his eyes.

Jake came speeding into the campground, almost hitting his friends before he slammed on his brakes next to the fire. They all quickly ran for their lives. The boys thought it was a dumb joke, but the girls did not think it was very funny. As they were coming back toward Jake, they all became very concerned when they saw his face.

"Jake, where is Rex?" asked Alice, starting to get scared.

"Hey man, what the hell is going on?" asked Ben, getting angry.

"H–he is re–real. Smi–ling J–ack is real," said Jake.

All their faces went white as the fire went out by a gust of wind. Alice quickly turned on her flashlight and saw the rest of them doing the same as she looked back to see Jake, but he was gone. She made her way to his four-wheeler, and as she got closer, she saw a giant puddle of blood next to it. She followed it to a tree. As she followed the tree up to its branches with her flashlight, she saw Jake's body hanging with his guts dangling from his stomach.

She screamed at the site of his body and took several steps back, until her friends shined their flashlights over on her, making her jump while looking at them. She sighed with relief once she noticed it was them. But her friends had a different face for Smiling Jack was right behind her. Alice quickly turned around to see him as he put the anchor straight through her and ripped it right out.

The three other friends panicked. They ran for their four-wheelers and peeled out, heading down the mountain as fast as they could, running for their lives. Ben and Lucy went around the first bend fine, then Carol came around, and Smiling Jack was standing in the middle of the dirt road. Carol swerved off the road into the forest, getting impaled by a branch that killed him. Ben and Lucy kept heading down the road as fast as they could until their four-wheelers died on them.

*"What is going on?"* asked Lucy, who was scared out of her mind.

"I don–" Ben quit talking when he saw Smiling Jack down the road.

Smiling Jack tilted his head at Ben and Lucy before he started running straight at them. Both of them panicked and ran into the woods. Ben stopped after running for a couple of yards and hid under a tree. Lucy kept on running, hitting a steep part of the mountain. She lost her footing and fell down the mountain.

As she was rolling down the mountain, she bounced off the ground and into the air. As she was going down, Smiling Jack came out from behind a tree and swung the anchor, cutting her in half. Her body flew two different directions down the mountain.

Ben lay down on the tree, waiting for the sun to rise while hoping for the nightmare to be over. He froze and began to sweat when he felt something breathing behind him. He slowly turned around to see nothing at all, but the breathing was still there.

He slowly started to crawl backward out from under the tree when suddenly a rotten hand came out from the dark and grabbed his leg. He screamed as he was sucked underneath the tree.

#  GLOBAL DISEASE

t was three years since the virus had come out and we were still on quarantine. The government said it was unsafe still. We were not allowed to leave the house except for the essential employees. The only way we could get our goods was when the military came and dropped them off once a week. Sometimes there was not enough food so we had to ration it to make it last. We were only allowed to have power for five hours a day, every other day. They said we must sacrifice some for all of us to live. If we were caught outside, there would be severe consequences. I had never seen what they were until that day.

It was a normal Tuesday with my little boy Nephi. He was always full of energy, even on the days he was not able to eat. We were building a fort in his bedroom for the thousandth time, trying to make him happy, when all he really wanted was to go outside and play in the grass. After we built our fort, we made lunch. He got six beans and a quarter of a roll to eat.

I sat down with him and watched him eat. I held onto my stomach for it was hurting from how hungry I was. My son looked into my eyes, and I knew he could sense my pain so he gave up his roll for me. I took it and ate it slowly as tears ran down my eyes for how amazing my son was.

We lay down to take a nap like normal because we didn't have a lot of energy.

Once I woke up, I went to get my son out of his bed so we could hang out and read a book together. But I noticed something. The front door was open. My heart quickly dropped to my stomach and I ran to the door. He was playing in the front yard, chasing a butterfly. I screamed for him to come back inside. He looked at me with such joy in his face that I had never seen before. Then the military vehicles pulled into our yard.

Soldiers came out with guns, swarming my yard and aiming right at my son. An officer shouted at me to go back inside. I closed the door and went to my window, pushing my face against it in fear of what would happen to my son. They threw him in the back of an enclosed five-ton truck. As they threw him in, I got to see his face. It was full of fear that I had never seen before.

As they locked it up, one of the military men walked over to the side and hit a switch. Right at that moment, my heart stopped beating as I saw flames inside the vehicle. I began to hit the wall until my hands were bleeding. I fell to my knees for I couldn't stand because my body was shaking in anger.

I heard a loud beeping and heard a voice. "We had another patient that had just died. People, please stay inside. It is too dangerous to be out. If we all work together, we will get through this and we will all survive if you follow what you are told. Thank you, and have a nice day."

# OTTO

Up on the sixth floor lived a gentleman named Otto. Otto used to be a party clown for kids' birthdays. He called himself Otto the amazing clown. That is, until one night when he ended up catching on fire, getting third-degree burns all over his body and losing all his hair. After that, his life went downhill. The only time he left his house was at night when he went to the convenience store to get alcohol.

As the sun went down and the moon was out, Otto would put on his hoody and head out for the night. He opened his door while slowly peeking out to make sure it was clear. He headed straight for the stairs for he feared the elevator. He moved fast to avoid any contact with people until he made it out into the alleyway.

He took deep breaths, feeling his anxiety go away. Looking at the moon and smiling was the only thing that gave him happiness anymore.

He made his way to the back of the convenience store where a semi was parked, unloading its cargo. He waited for his moment. Once the coast was clear, he snagged a couple of cases of beer and then bounced back to the alleyway to head back home.

Right as he went for the handle to enter the apartments, the door swung open, hitting him, knocking all his beer out of his hands, and spilling it into the alleyway. He panicked and tried to save what he could, but it wasn't much. Three young men came walking out laughing at him. He could tell they were not from this area by looking at their clothes and smelling their cologne. They were from uptown. One of the guys went for his hoody to remove it, but Otto hit away his hand in anger.

The three men's attitude quickly changed, and they all began to push him and kick him to the ground until they saw his face and took a few steps back in disgust. Blood was dripping down his face as stumbled to get up.

"Please stop," he whispered to them.

The three of them ran away as Otto reached out his hand. They hopped into an old-school red Mustang, leaving Otto in the alleyway. As he got his footing, he grabbed the handle to the building, swung it wide-open, and then ran up the stairs. Once he made it to his apartment, he slammed the door behind him and fell to his knees crying.

After a moment of getting himself together, he crawled over to his living room and opened a vent, pulling out his emergency whiskey bottle. He popped off the top and chugged it down. Once he finished the bottle, he made his way to the bathroom. He put his hands on the counter to hold himself up, and then he looked at all the blood on his face.

Instead of crying, he laughed uncontrollably. He whipped the blood off his face and used it to put a smile on the mirror before he punched it, shattering the glass. The apartment went dead silent as he made his way to his bedroom. He got out his old clown costume, slipped into the multicolor jumpsuit, and slid on his big red feet.

He left his room and headed to the kitchen where he grabbed several cloths, tying them up throughout the apartment and putting the last on his gas stove. He turned on the stove, catching it on fire. He slowly made his way out to the hallway, leaving the door wide-open with the smoke following him as he went down the stairs to the alleyway. Otto stood there watching it burn till the fire department showed up.

He was walking down street as police kept driving past to go help, when he noticed a garage door was wide-open. And he saw an axe lying there. He grabbed the axe and continued to make his way through the neighborhoods until he reached the rich area. Otto stopped in front of a giant white house with a red Mustang.

He entered the house slowly, skulking around when he heard a TV upstairs. He made his way to see the same young man who had beat him lying there on his bed while enjoying a show without a care in the world. Otto did not hesitate. He rushed into the room, and before the young man could do anything, Otto knocked him out. He dragged him down the stairs, threw him into the Mustang, and drove off into the night.

The young man woke up in a middle of an abandoned house. He tried to scream but was gagged. He looked around to find a way out when suddenly lights flashed, blinding him for a second. As his vision came back, he saw the burned man in a clown costume.

"Hello. I am Otto the clown. Do you want to see a magic trick?"

The young man shook his head with his wide blue eyes. Otto ignored him, pulling out three bowling balls and tossing them into the air to juggle. The first one came down, hitting the young man in the head, cracking his skull. The young man screamed in pain while shaking the chair.

"How about a balloon for you, buddy?" asked Otto, laughing out of control.

Otto turned around while twisting a balloon. Once all done, he turned to show the kid a dog. As he got closer with it, he popped it and gas enveloped the young man. That was when Otto pulled out a lighter, tossed it on him, and then pushed the chair back to break it. The young man began to run for his life until he fell into some water. As he pulled himself out, he screamed in pain as he got third-degree burns all over him. As he looked back at Otto, he ran for it, but when he went outside, he was shot twice by his two friends.

They walked up to look at his lifeless body.

"Go check the building to see if he is OK," said the one with a gun.

He ran into the building screaming for his friend when he felt a sharp pain in his back. Otto put the axe into his back, then he put his foot on his back breaking the axe free. The kid dropped to the ground. Otto lost control and continued to swing the axe at him, all the while laughing. But when he heard a voice, he quickly went into the shadows, waiting as the last one came walking in swinging his gun around screaming for his friends.

He kept screaming their names until he saw his buddy on the ground bleeding out. As he was about to speak, an axe come flying, hitting him straight in the head. Otto ripped out the axe, and as he looked at the body, he began to laugh. Then he walked away into the night.

# THE LITTLE FAIRY

t was Halloween night, and three friends rode their bikes to an old burned house. The first to make it there was Jake, who was fifteen. He was the most athletic of the group. With a brown mullet, blue eyes, and olive skin, most of the girls thought he was dreamy.

The two twin brothers came pulling up right behind him. Nick was heavyset while Mike looked like a twig, as if Nick ate all the food in the house. The only thing they had in common was that they both had blond hair with green eyes and crooked teeth with mayo-looking skin.

The trio stood in front of the house at the edge of the sidewalk. They all looked at each other, and Jake with a smile across his face asked, "Are you ready to meet the little fairy?"

The twin brothers both swallowed and nodded as they followed Jake to the house. As they got closer, all they could smell was burned wood, as if it had freshly been on fire. As Jake took his first step on the porch, a giant wave of dust shot straight up into the air. Jake waved it away as he walked across the burned deck. As they walked by the first window, they could see all the furniture in the house still melted to the floor.

As they pushed the door open, it made a creaking sound. They all stood at the entranceway a little afraid to keep going. Jake shook his whole body as he tried to get rid of the chills and took a couple of steps in, looking around a little more before he told his friends to follow him up the stairs.

After they reached the top, they headed straight into a room.

It was a little girl's room with dolls, a playhouse, and a drawing table all melted and destroyed. In the middle of the room was a pile of ash where a young girl was burned alive. Jake walked to it, picking up some of the ash as some fell through his fingers.

"Put it back, Jake. This doesn't feel right," said Mike.

"Now you want to back out? Now that we are here? We are going to do this. Aren't you tired of being a nobody? This is our chance, man."

"But what if the curse is real? What if she comes back from the dead?" asked Nick.

"Dude, it's just a myth. The older kids make a pile every year and make the new guys do it to see if they have what it takes. And I am doing all the work, so I don't know why you two are so afraid."

"I am sorry, man. I can't do this. I just can't," said Nick, raising his arms and heading out the door.

Jake followed trying to stop him. As Jake took a step out of the room they heard a little girl crying. The trio looked back to see a little girl with red hair and a fairy dress. They all stood there too scared to move, all of them going ghostly white. The little girl slowly looked up at the boys' faces and had a scene of terror as the girl had no eyes and half her face was burned, showing bone.

Her wings on her back began to move, lifting her into the air. As she opened her mouth, fiery ash came out. She charged at Mike, landing on top of him and vomiting fiery ash all over his face.

He screamed in pain. The other two boys didn't wait and ran down the stairs. As Jake made it halfway, he tripped, falling the rest of the away and losing all the ash in his hand. He looked up and through the door saw Nick out on the street riding on his bike. He looked back up the stairs because there was nothing but silence from upstairs now. He began to breathe heavily for the young girl's head was poking around the corner, but it was at the ceiling. She began to crawl around and up on the ceiling, slowly making it down till she was right above him. She made a huge smile, and ash fell from her mouth. Then a fire ring formed around Jake, but before he could do anything, she dropped from the ceiling, landing on him, and both vanished into the floor.

Nick pedaled his bike as fast as his body would let him go, when out of nowhere his front tire stopped, causing him to fly over his handlebars and roll on the ground. He looked up to see a hand coming out of the ground and holding his front tire. The girl from the house slowly came out of the ground, and Nick was too scared to move. Once she was fully out, she walked over to him very slowly, got to her knees, and vomited ash into his mouth.

Nick stood up, turned, and walked straight down the street as the girl stood there smiling. Nick entered a house where a bunch of teenagers were partying and drinking beer. When one of them noticed Nick walking in, he screamed, and it didn't take long before the rest of the group did too.

"So did you do it, little buddy? And where are the rest of your friends? Did they all bounce on you? To be completely honest, I didn't expect you to do it," said one of the teenagers.

Nick stood in silence, not moving an inch.

"Hey man, he asked you a question," said another.

That was when Nick turned around vomiting ash on the kid, catching him on fire. Everyone panicked and tried to get out, but all the doors were locked. Nick burst into flames, making the teenagers panic even more.

As they screamed, the little fairy girl watched outside as the house began to burn.

# COCKROACH

t was a late Tuesday afternoon when a father was coming home to his apartment where his three little girls were playing with old wooden blocks. When their dad walked through the door, the kids' eyes lit up with joy and they all ran to hug him while giggling. The father hugged them all tightly, holding back his tears as he looked at his place and how rundown it was.

As his kids let go, he put on a giant smile and took them to the kitchen where he cooked some noodles and hot dogs. They ate and laughed together and did homework together before going to bed, where the three of them slept together on one bed. Then he headed to the living room and sat down on the couch, where he looked around. He felt like a failure to his daughters.

He accidentally fell asleep on the couch, and when he woke up, he realized he was late for work and his girls were still asleep. He went into a panic getting them up and ready for school. But once everyone was ready and in the car, it would not start and they had to take the bus.

He finally got them to school and made it to work four hours late. Before he could even make it through the front door, his boss was waiting outside for him. His boss stopped him, informing him he was no longer needed and that this had happened too many times. The dad lost it, hitting the boss in the face, and once he had realized what he had done, he ran for it. After running several blocks, he collapsed to his knees and began to cry.

A stranger walked up to see if he was OK, and after they talked for a moment, he offered him a solution to his problem. He told him he can go to Mexico and sell his kidney for a lot of money. The guy offered his hand to help him up, telling him he would be home within two days. After staring at the ground and thinking about it, he took the guy's hand.

They made it to Mexico that night, where the doctor was waiting for him in a rundown building in the middle of nowhere. They laid him down on the table and put him to sleep. He woke up in the same building, but no one was around. He was bandaged up from where they took his kidney. It hurt for him to move, but he did, and as he looked around, he found a suitcase of money in the bathroom.

He began to cry with joy knowing for the first time in his life he would be able to give his girls a great life. He made it home to see his girls excited to see him after him being gone for so long. He took them out to dinner that night to the nicest restaurant he could find. They were having a great time eating and making jokes.

Suddenly out of nowhere, a cockroach fell onto the table. The father was confused how that landed there. When he looked at his daughters, their faces were pale as another cockroach was crawling out their father's nose. He panicked. He rushed to the bathroom to see what was going on.

As he looked into the mirror, he couldn't see anything unusual. But then his side began to hurt where the surgeons had operated. He quickly removed the bandages to see his skin move. He began to hit his side trying to kill whatever was inside him, when he felt pain behind his eye. He looked into the mirror to see his eyeballs slowly coming out of his head. One little tear came out when his eyes burst, and several cockroaches crawled out.

# WISHING WELL

There once was a well that would give you anything you ever dreamed about. The only thing was you had to give it something that you loved dearly. The bigger the sacrifice, the bigger the reward. A woman found it in the middle of a field where she gave up her favorite dress. When she got home, a diamond necklace that she had always wanted was on her dresser.

She leaped with joy and would do this often, especially to get something for her daughter for the holidays. Until one day when her father, who was her whole world, passed away. She could not bear another day without him so she took her daughter to the well. She gave her a big hug and a kiss and pushed her into the well.

When she got home later that day, her father was sitting on her couch waiting for her. Her heart filled with joy and for a while she was happy. But every time she walked past her daughter's room, her heart would break. She could not bear it anymore so she took her father to the well and pushed him in. Once she got home, her daughter was sitting on the couch waiting for her.

She would do this over and over with the two of them so she would never lose them. But each time she did it, they would lose more and more of their souls. They would become lifeless each time with no energy and would try to kill themselves. Until one day she took her father to the well to get her daughter back. She pushed him with a smile on her face. As she began to make her way out of the field, she heard a soft whisper from the well.

"Kassssssssey."

She returned to the well out of curiosity, and as she got closer, the voice got louder, and louder, saying her name.

"Kasssssssssey."

And it continued until she was at the well. Then it went silent and she stared down the dark hole.

Suddenly her father and daughter came popping out of the well and dragged her back into it with them.

# WEREWOLF IN SHEEPSKIN

I t was a full moon, and a man was walking down the street with his dog. They took a trail that led him down by some ponds. He loved going down there on a full moon night and staring at the reflection of the moon on the lake. He took a seat on the bench that was right by a weeping willow. Then he noticed a figure standing across the pond, and it was staring right at him.

It began to make him feel uncomfortable so he decided to leave. As he walked, the figure stared at him the whole time. Eventually he ran for it with his dog as he was getting the creeps. He kept on running until he was out of sight and stopped to catch his breath. Then his dog began to growl at the dark.

The man felt a chill go down his spin when someone came walking out of the dark into the light. He was wearing a black trench coat and a black cowboy hat. As the man looked up, there was something wrong with his face. It had three mouths, two noses, and five eye sockets. They were all sewed on together, and it appeared they had all come from different people.

As the dog kept growling, the man in the trench coat let out a bark that sounded just like a dog. The dog whimpered and ran off, the human too much in shock to hold his dog's leash. The trench coat man took his hat off, showing more of his face. There were even more people's faces sewed on. And then he took his trench coat off. He had nothing underneath it, and what the man saw was terrifying. He looked like he was wearing a jumpsuit of human skin that was sewed together.

The naked man howled at the moon. He grabbed the back of his head and removed the skin from him, showing that he really was a werewolf. He stood there staring at the man, growing to over eight feet tall. Mainly black with red throughout his fur. He got on all four legs and slowly made his way with a smile, showing his sharp, long fangs.

As he got right into the man's face, he said, "You are perfect for what I need."

The man took a deep swallow right before the werewolf killed him. The werewolf dragged the body into his cave where he had hundreds of human body skins lying around. He began to skin the body and then took it to the sewing machine where made a new human jumpsuit. He took hours combining it with others he had and putting teeth around the neck into the skin to make it look like a necklace.

Once it was completed, he threw it on and walked to a mirror. He loved the skin tones that he had, making his eyes pop. He grabbed his trench coat and stopped in front of the mirror one last time before leaving. He headed out of his cave into the forest where he could see bright lights in the distant sky. He strolled over there. And as he entered, there were thousands of werewolves wearing human skin, for it was a fashion show party.

As he made his way through the crowds, other werewolves were buying humans in cages to make new skins and others were selling premade human-skin jumpsuits. He headed to the back of a building where a handful of werewolves were getting ready to walk down the runway to show their new clothing lines. He waited for the curtains to open to make his big reveal.

# CHRISTMAS NIGHT

I t was a snowy Christmas night and little Henry and Jackie wanted to stay up to see Santa Claus. They waited on the couch with a flashlight until midnight. Then they heard a big thud from the roof! They both hurried into the hall to wait and see. They sat there in silence until they heard him say, "Ho, ho, ho."

They jumped out into the living room to get Santa, when they quickly realized that something was wrong. Santa was not human but a giant cookie. Instead of eating the cookie, he attached it to his body making it a part of him. He sat on the couch and took what looked like an old piece from him. Santa began to reshape it like a small man.

Once he was done, it came to life jumping with joy as it ran up into the chimney. Santa began to put down the presents when he heard a thud. One of the children had dropped their flashlight. He turned and smiled at them as his frosted beard dripped from his cookie face.

Santa went to his bag, opened it, and laid it on the ground. The children, still too scared to move, looked at the bag while waiting. Suddenly a creature that was not from this world came out. It had no eyes, sharp fangs, long, skinny arms and legs, and its body was like an accordion the way it was able to stretch. The children screamed and ran for their lives as it chased them through the house. As the kids tried to make it to their parents' room the creature ate them all, not leaving a trace. It crawled back in its sack. Santa said, "Ho, ho, ho," before going back up the chimney to go to the next house.

# GRANDMA'S STEW

A young man and woman were chained up in the garage, dangling from the ceiling. The man's two legs were cut off, and he was slowly losing blood. The woman still had her legs and kept kicking trying to find a way out to save them. She swung her feet up on a beam trying to break it when she heard a noise from outside.

It was an old lady walking in. She made her way to the workbench, grabbing a chainsaw. She then begged her not to, but the little old lady ignored her and cut off her two legs anyway. As they dropped to the floor, the young woman passed out from the pain. The old lady picked them up, put them into a bag, and went back into the house.

She went straight to the kitchen and cut them into smaller pieces, and then she threw them into her stew. Then she tossed in some potatoes, onions, and other veggies. Once she was done, she made three bowls and called for the children. They came running and after sitting down ate the stew.

Then one of them asked, "When will Mom and Dad be home, Grandma?"

"Soon, little one. Keep eating so you can be as big and strong like them," Grandma replied.

The two children smiled and kept eating their stew.

#  MY NEW PET

Theo was a young man who had always wanted a pet. His mom had always told him no. But on his birthday, his mom got him a new robot. Theo was not pleased. He would always kick it downhill or leave it at a park. But this loyal robot would come home every night ready to please his master.

Then one evening Theo had the robot hop into the dumpster and told it to wait there for him. Theo stood there and waited so he could watch as the robot got dumped and smashed and taken to the dump. But he was still "alive" and found his way home to play with Theo.

But he saw that Theo's mother had replaced him with a dog. Something right there turned a switch on the robot that made him very angry. When Theo went to the school the next day, the robot broke into the house, found the dog, and killed it, putting the dog's skin on his body.

When Theo got home to play with his dog, all he found was blood. As he followed it upstairs, his robot was waiting for him, sitting on his mother's bed while wearing the dog's skin. And he had Theo's mother on a leash and a ball in her mouth.

"Hello, Theo. I have been waiting for you," the robot said as he tossed a leash to the boy. "You're going to be my new pet. And you're going to be a good boy." Theo put on the leash and the robot took him to the top of the stairs, where he kicked him down and watched him lie at the bottom crying.

#  RED BEARD

hree friends were sitting by a campfire telling scary stories. When it was Carl's turn, he said, "Have you ever heard of Red Beard?"

The others said no.

Carl continued. "He was a vicious outlaw. Tale has it that he was almost seven feet tall with long, brown hair and a beard down to his chest that was bright red from the blood of all the people he killed with his handmade axes. They say he was missing his left eyeball. One night rangers surrounded the cabin he was staying in that night and burned it to the ground. They waited for screams, but instead it was laughter of a mad man. He did not stop laughing until he died. The rangers celebrated that night getting drunk until they passed out, leaving the fire still burning. Little did they know that doing that doomed them all because Red Beard himself came crawling out and killed them all before dragging them to hell. It is said today that if you ever leave a fire burning with no one watching he will come from hell and kill everyone until the sun comes back up."

They all just burst out laughing at Carl. "Dude, that was the lamest story ever!" shouted his buddy Chucky.

"It's a story a park ranger would talk about for fire safety," William said.

Carl laughed it off with them as he did not believe the story himself; it was something he heard as a kid once.

As it got late, William and Chucky went to bed, leaving Carl to kill the fire. He dumped the water on it, and as the smoke cleared, he noticed a little bit was still burning but he shrugged it off thinking it would die out in a couple of minutes. So he tossed the bucket next to his chair and headed to bed.

As all three passed out, the embers became brighter and brighter. A hand came out of the ash and a man began to pull himself through it. It was Red Beard standing over the fire, breathing heavily. He pulled out his axes, and then he walked to the first tent, where he slaughtered William. But not before he screamed for his life.

Chucky and Carl came out of their tents to see what was going on and saw Red Beard standing with William's body dangling over his shoulder. Red Beard tossed him to the ground and spun the axes in his hands. Both boys turned and sprinted to the trees.

Red Beard whistled and his horse came out of the ash. Red Beard hopped on and began to chase them.

They both split, hoping to have a chance to make it. Chucky climbed a tree to wait it out up there until daylight. But Red Beard was able to find him quickly as he sat on his horse staring at Chucky with a grin. Red Beard put his hand on the tree, and fire burst from his hands as he started to climb it.

Chucky was trapped and began to panic when he jumped twenty feet from a branch, landing on a log and breaking his legs. He lay there screaming in pain as Red Beard slowly made his way over to him and began to swing his axes, killing Chucky. Once he was done, Red Beard tossed him on his horse to find Carl.

Carl found a cave and hid in the back waiting for daylight. He heard footsteps above him, and his body tightened up. He even held his breath hoping that would help him out. After a few seconds, they went away. He made a giant gasp for air. That was when he saw the sun's light and his heart began to pound. He ran to his car.

He slid to his car door, opening it and jumping in as he tried to start the engine. It would not turn over. As he looked around in fear, he noticed his two friends' lifeless bodies in the back. Before he could react, there was a thud on the hood of the car. Carl jumped out of his seat to see Red Beard. He began to shake his head for it couldn't be, but he realized that the sun was only halfway up. Red Beard whistled to his horse and pulled the car with a rope tied to the bumper of the car into the firepit. Red Beard sat there at the fire and waited for the sun to come completely out, and then he vanished back to hell.

# MOTHER'S LOVE

A sweet mother and two of her children came home after hitting the pharmacy. The kids went to play and the mother pulled out her new pills that her doctor had prescribed. She took two as told and then took a quick nap as normal.

She woke up to get the kids and make dinner before her husband got home.

She found them playing like normal and was about to tell them to come inside but noticed two white creatures standing next to the clothesline. They were tall and white with big, black eyes and long fangs. The mother panicked, picking her kids up and taking them upstairs.

The two creatures followed the mother, but she stopped them by slamming the door into their faces. It was not for long before they began to bang on the door trying to get in. The mother put the two kids into a closet and then searched for a weapon to fight them off. She found a bat, picked it up, and stepped in front of the closet ready to protect her children.

The banging stopped, the door handle slowly opened, and both creatures stood there with their heads tilted, staring at her for a moment before they attacked. She swung, hitting one of them in the head and killing it as the other went for her foot. It began to drag her down the stairs but she kicked it off, giving her time to stand up. As it went back up, she swung, hitting it down the stairs with the fall killing it.

As she was about to get her children out, she heard noises from outside, and as she looked, she saw more of the creatures in the streets. She ran into the closet with the two children, sat in the dark, and waited for her husband to get home.

It felt like days in the dark waiting for him to show up. She heard a door open and heard his voice shouting for them. Her heart leaped for joy when she heard him scream in pain.

She feared those creatures would get him so she couldn't sit and leave him. She ran out of the closet to the stairs, where he was holding their son at the bottom of the stairs. Her face went white as she looked over to the corner where the creature was actually her daughter. She panicked and ran to the closet to see what was in there.

As she investigated the closet to see if her two kids were still in there, she discovered they were. They were crying in the closet. She turned around slowly, confused as to what was going on, and as she did, three figures were standing there: her husband and their two kids. She stood frozen for she did not know what to believe anymore.

When a third figure came up the stairs, it was another one of those creatures standing behind her family. Its body began to change into her and walked forward with a smile on her face. It got closer and closer till it was right in her face.

"This is our home now," she said.

# THE SKIN

One day out in the swamp, a group of rednecks left their boat and was playing around in the mud. One of them stumbled upon something and called the others to check it out. It was a giant dead reptile. But this reptile was not like anything they had ever seen before. It looked as if it walked on its back legs, so they decided to throw it in their boat and take it home.

They laid it on a table in their shed and decided to cut it open to see what it looked like inside. As they were doing that, one of them got squirted in the face with a liquid. Everyone there laughed at him as they kept pulling out all the guts to check it all out. Once they were done, they tossed the guts and kept the skin. One of them wanted to hang it on the wall.

Later that night, the man who got sprayed with liquid all over his face couldn't stop sweating and was tossing and turning in his bed. He was hearing voices in his head telling him to come home. He tried to fight it until they got so loud in his head he finally stood up. He didn't know why, but he headed to the shed where they had earlier gutted the unknown reptile. He went inside and began to undress. Then he put on the reptile skin, and finally he sewed himself inside it.

Once fully sewed inside, he walked out into the middle of the yard. Suddenly a giant beam of light hit him from the sky. It was so bright it woke up his friends. They went running outside to see what was going on, only to see their friend in reptile skin being taken up into the sky.

He looked down upon his friends with joy.

"They chose. They want me to lead them! They want me to be part of their world!" he shouted as he ascended into the sky.

Printed in the United States
by Baker & Taylor Publisher Services